The Zafranama

ISBN 9781927028162

The Zafranama

By Vikram Dasa

*

Myths and legends are carried from the past of the revolts and struggles against the corporate tyrants who now rule in the East and West. No one can really say if any of it is true. There is very little to verify or support the stories that have been passed down orally from outlaw to another. The ancient books from the old world were destroyed in the East, and history had been erased so that it could be rewritten, rearranged, and repurposed to suit a new kind of tyranny—the kind of tyranny that didn't try to destroy or control its enemy but instead divided, diluted, crushed and assimilated like a great boa constrictor. When a few Christians from the old world survived the Great War and began to preach the contents of the real Bible, the ruling castes didn't feed them to the lions or try to torture them like the Romans had once done. They let them do that to themselves. They simply created and sponsored other Christian sects with slightly different interpretations of a slightly different Bible that fully embraced Athman Caste Society. They gave these new Christians wealth and media coverage and built their temples so that they overshadowed the old Christians who denied caste and who tried to end caste slavery. All of these new sects preached a message close to the original message of the Bible except for one detail. A detail that was everything to the ruling castes. These newly created Christians all accepted Athman Caste Society without question or doubt as if caste had always been a part of the Bible and Christianity. And this was indeed everything to those who controlled Aryana.

Not one Christian in the new sects preached against Caste Apartheid. Not one. They all supported Caste Apartheid and maintained that Jesus himself was an Aryan-Athman, a living god like all the other Athmans, and that he openly practiced caste slavery in the name of the 'divine' society. To the original Christians this was ludicrous. Nothing could be further from the truth. But no one listened to the real Christians from the old world. Not anymore. The real Christians from the old world were stigmatized as extremists for denying something as 'natural' and 'sacred' as caste hierarchy as defined by Athman Caste Society. The real Christians of Old were ridiculed for having tried to convince the newly created Christians that they had never believed in Caste Apartheid and that anyone who subscribed to any version of Christianity that embraced caste slavery and oppression was not a real Christian. These 'radicals' tried to protect and conserve the original message of the Bible, but it was no use. The Christians of Old were outnumbered, silenced, and, when they had been properly diluted in number and message, they were secretly hunted down and 'disappeared' during the Aryan Reclamation.

This was how it was with all the old religions that denied Caste Apartheid. Eventually the leaders of the old religions banded together and religious wars broke between the old and the new within the Empire. The Athmans gave full support to their sects and drove out those they did not 'disappear'. What followed was a crusade to incinerate all links to the past that did not support Caste Apartheid. The real Buddhists gave the longest fight. They were used to the ruling castes meddling with their history as they had been protecting their message of equality for centuries. But this time they were overpowered. The Buddhists of Old tried to remind everyone that Buddhism began as an absolute rebellion and denial of caste slavery. But for every real Buddhist that spoke in this manner, a dozen false Buddhists, sponsored by the Empire, called them separatists and denounced them as extremists on the massive television screens overlooking the streets of Aryana. There was little they could do to counter the propaganda set against them, and all who protested against Caste Apartheid were stigmatized as 'extremists'.

By the time the ruling castes had destroyed all documents that proved historical rebellion and resistance to caste, by the time they were through creating new interpretations of old religions, all the old religions had been crushed and assimilated and all religions were completely in line with Athman Caste Society, though they may have had different Gods, places of worship, prophets and sacred texts. This the ruling castes didn't care about. They didn't care about gods and prophets and temples. They only cared about the system that maintained their power, and so long as a religion didn't contradict their power structure, they were left alone to believe in whatever god they wanted.

And it is true. No one within the walls of the Empire remembered a time when these old religions had been born in heresy. Born as a reaction to caste slavery and spiritual oppression maintained by lies preached as religion. Those who tried to remember or rebel against the Athmans were eliminated in the camps during the Aryan Revival and Reclamation. Those who survived the Reclamation hid in the Deadlands and sought out Sundri and her infamous outlaws for help and understanding. It's also interesting to note that it wasn't only the religious books that were destroyed or repurposed to suite Athman Caste Society. It

7

was anything and everything.

Anything and everything that showed that there had once been rebellions against Caste Apartheid was attacked. Movies. Novels. Poems. Songs. Music videos. Comic books. All of it destroyed or reimagined in service of the 'divine' society that made gods out of one caste and slaves out of another. Like a massive python the ruling castes did as they had done since the dawn of time—

Crush and assimilate.

Instead of trying to ban rebellion or religion they flooded the Empire with counter religions and rebellions, movements close to the original but with conflicting messages and interpretations when it came to caste. Thousands upon thousands of cults, sects and religions distracted and divided by inconsistencies and petty differences; yet, all of them, perfectly aligned with Athman Caste Society. It was brilliant. It was the best kind of tyranny. The most effective kind. The ideological kind. A spiritual tyranny to be studied and understood.

The ruling castes didn't have to destroy their enemies. They just had to confuse them. Keep them fighting with themselves while they erased everything and anything that compromised their power structure. And this was how it was within the Great Wall of the Empire. But not outside.

Outside the Great Wall the outlaws still searched for truth.

*

Dawn was a tinge of orange and red in the East, and the air already began to shimmer in the heat. The old librarian led the outlaws through the shanties and ruins of the Deadlands. His name was Banda Singh. He had been searching the Deadlands for the last thirty years for truth—for artifacts and sacred texts from the old world. He was tall, supple, broad-shouldered and strong as steel from his experience as a RAD agent. He had been a secret guardian of the Empire in a former life, a life he barely remembered, a life he tried to forget. His face was scarred from his days fighting against the outlaws and his hair, which he kept in a thick black turban protected by chakkar quoits, was long and white like his beard. His dark eyes were strong and alert despite his age, and he wore a kirpan over a dark robe made of black leather and kromo-steel, which he had salvaged from his old RAD uniform and dead comrades. To most he was a Sikh of Old who, unlike the Sikhs of the Empire, had forfeited his caste last name for the communal Singh that spoke neither of caste nor status but of community and equality and the promise of action—not silence or indifference-- in the face of tyranny. Though he had spent the first part of his life trying to change history, change the message of his religion, he was one of the few who still remembered and respected this long forgotten aspect of the Sikh baptismal ceremony. The rejection of Caste Apartheid for equal society. The forfeiting of the caste name for the communal name. In fact to his interpretation this declaration of community and equality was perhaps the main focus of

Sikh baptismal ceremony. But not anymore.

Now this act of rebellion to caste oppression had been erased, universally and conveniently forgotten as Sikhs of the Empire enjoyed the ego and benefits that came with their caste names. Sikhs of the Empire, Banda reflected, were not Sikhs. They were something else, but definitely not Sikhs. Many even partook in caste oppression and tyranny. To his disgust many Sikhs of Empire traded in slaves and sold slaves to the ruling castes and the television networks for their gratuitous coliseum fights and their Kalidasa Games where slaves fought to the death and their memories were harvested for their precious 'Kalima' drugs, an upper caste drug that the rich could use to experience the death of a slave and feel the exhilaration of death without actually dying. A drug to help those who suffered from too much to escape their utter boredom and feel alive through the death of another. Some upper caste Sikhs, to Banda's disgust, even ran Kali-Bongs or K-Bongs as they were called. These K-bongs were the epitome of evil. They were sanctioned establishments where upper castes could rent a booth and a slave and do whatever they wanted to the slave to relieve themselves of the frustrations and anxieties that came with living a meaningless life. Nothing was banned, nothing was out of reach, nothing was off-limits, not even murder, and murder wasn't even that bad compared to the things the upper castes did to these rented slaves for their amusement; and if they murdered them, if things got a little out of hand in a K-bong booth as they often did, the Athman in question merely had to pay for the dead slave, or replace them with a slave of their own. Lechers and untouchables—the Shudra and the Brahmans—were not to be treated as people with rights and laws, but as spiritual lepers there to serve and be cleansed by the Athmans for the next life.

When some protests began against the K-bongs, the Athmans immediately classified the K-Bong ritual as an act of Sati even greater than the immolation of a widow on her husband's funeral pyre that would cleanse her dead husband of any sin he might have committed against the ruling castes; or the ritualistic sacrifice of children which had returned to the Empire in great force when slaves were deemed cheaper than pumpkins and more in line with the sacred texts which demanded the blood of an innocent child for the goddess Kali.

Banda shuddered at the thought. False Sikhs sold slaves like pumpkins to the temples and the K-Bongs and they did so believing they were serving some higher purpose and hierarchy that had always been a part of their religion. These slaves, they believed, would be purified and in the next life and they would come back at a higher level of consciousness and therefore a higher level on the Athman caste ladder. It was an economical system for the rulers. No promises in the immediate life for service and sacrifice. But promises in spades for the next life.

Banda didn't know exactly when caste returned to Sikhs, but he knew that it had not come in the new world during the Aryan Reclamation when all other religions were properly assimilated into Aryan-Athman Caste Society. The change had come in the old world like the Buddhists, though the Buddhists had managed to retain some truth of their rejection of caste. Toward the end of the 20th century the ruling castes had divided and diluted and disappeared all documents and leaders who held on to the truth about caste rebellion in the Sikh religion in order to assimilate Sikhs into their 'society'. It was as though the first words of the Guru who had given Sikhs their uniform had not been against caste tyranny. It was as though the first words of the Guru hadn't been against the caste system or the oppression of the Hill Rajas and the ruling castes. It was as though the Guru hadn't forfeited his caste name for the communal name he had given his Sikhs. By all historical records in the Empire--he hadn't.

In the Empire the last Sikh guru was always referred to as Guru Gobind Singh Rai, and he had been declared an Athman who had adopted Rai and not forfeited Rai at the Sikh baptismal ceremony in 1699. Everything was remembered about the ceremony except the first words spoken of the Guru after he had baptized the first five Sikhs as supposed protectors of the ruling castes. Somehow the new Sikhs of the Empire actually believed that they took on caste names at the ceremony. Somehow the meaning of the ceremony had been reversed so that only the aesthetic survived.

But Banda, whose job as a RAD agent had been propaganda and assimilation for the Athmans, had found other interpretations of history. He had found the old documents, those that contradicted this idea that the Guru supported Caste Apartheid and had adopted a caste name as proof undeniable. Documents that had not been incinerated or destroyed during the Golden Temple siege when the upper castes had attacked the most sacred temple of the Sikhs with an entire army.

Banda still had the quotes of his Guru asking for Sikhs to forfeit their last name as the final blow to caste oppression—as the final act of baptism. The act of dropping the caste name that not only made equals of all but asked Sikhs to forgo their egos. According to the old texts he had found, and completely opposite to ruling caste versions of history, the Guru was then baptized by his Sikhs and in his final act, he, too, dropped his last name and was from that moment on an equal to his community known as Guru

Gobind Singh Ji. Not Guru Gobind Singh Rai as the ruling castes had the new Sikhs believe with their history. Anyone who said differently was called an extremist who wanted to hurt the 'divine' society and threaten peace and stability.

Banda had more than the old quotes and documents as proof. He had military documents as well; and with these documents he could almost pinpoint to a year the moment this change in thought and message had come to Sikhs. The year when everything changed and the upper castes had finally put down a rebellion to Caste Apartheid that had begun centuries ago with a ceremony that had an entire community reject caste oppression and inequality by the mere act of dropping their caste names. The year the upper castes burned all of one leader's speeches against caste and attacked the Sikh Golden Temple to incinerate anything and everything that contradicted their power structure.

1984.

The military and school records said it all. These records the ruling castes had not fully destroyed, and as a RAD agent Banda had found them all, and analyzed them, and was putting together his own timeline and version of history. He had salvaged the records and could see that change printed right there on the yellowing papers printed hundreds of years ago.

War records showed that not a signal baptized Sikh enlisted donned a last name. Not a single one. Not a single baptized Sikh possessed a last name. All of them were Singhs.

This was true of the Boer War, World War One, and World War Two, and this was true all the way up to the Nineteen Eighties. Then, something happened. Something changed. The crushing and assimilation began in a way that could not be stopped or countered.

The old generation was wiped out so the new generation—lost and confused—could be assimilated.

The old records clearly showed a change in thought and message. Caste was returning to Sikhs in full force, as if dropping the caste name had never been part of the Sikh baptismal ceremony, as if the Guru's first words during the ceremony hadn't been for equality and justice, as if the Guru had never dropped his own caste name along with the entire congregation. Erased. Just like that. 1984.

And for Banda it wasn't too hard to track or draw his own conclusions. He could prove it to any outlaw who asked. He would just show them the records. Military records. Pre-84. Post-84. Showing them, they would see the truth for themselves.

Pre-84 almost every baptized Sikhs shared one last name. Post-84 last names were back with a vengeance along with caste inequality in the villages, homes, and gurdwaras. And it was when the change was complete, when the documents were incinerated, and a generation had been exterminated in the holiest temple of the Sikhs, that the Sikhs could be left alone to fight amongst themselves. They no longer posed a real threat to the upper caste power structure. Those who still maintained rebelling against caste oppression was a big part of the baptismal ceremony were silenced and stigmatized and consequently ignored as the change took root and became the new Sikh history.

Now the new Sikhs could be properly assimilated into the caste fold and the upper castes could move on to other threats such as the Muslims in Cashmere or Christians in Orissa who were breaking the anti-conversion laws and converting citizens out of caste oppression and paying the ultimate price for it. This was all long ago, before the collapse of governments and the corporate wars and the desperate scramble for resources that followed. Banda sighed deeply as he led the outlaws. It was more than just the registered names in the military records. It was the record of historical battles of the original Sikhs. Pre-84 history showed that the Sikhs had just as many battles with the Hill Rajas and ruling castes as they did with Islamic extremists who sought conversion by sword. After the storming and shellacking of the Golden Temple the former was no longer published or discussed while the latter was exaggerated and published everywhere. Upper castes used one defeated enemy to go against their current enemy by fueling the fires of hatred between Sikhs and Muslims. The history printed post-84 focused solely on the battles the gurus had with Islamic tyrants, but not the ruling caste tyrants who used religion to enslave the untouchables or to justify the use children for their strange caste rituals that were now openly practiced in the K-bongs and Athman Temples of the Empire. Ritual sacrifices that had for a time required pumpkins instead of children to avoid bad press and international scandal. All that changed, of course, with the Collapse and Aryan Reclamation when the ruling castes obtained complete control of press and society. When bad press and international scandal was no longer an issue and anyone outside the Great Wall was dismissed as a lecher.

It was strange. It was as though that part of history had never happened. It was as though the Sikhs had never taken issue with caste oppression. It was as though Sikhs had never rebelled against Caste Apartheid; or banned Sati; or Devadasi, which turned young low caste girls into sexual slaves to serve the living gods in their temples. No. This never happened. This rebellion against upper caste oppression by the Sikhs was just a whispered lie from the past by 'extremists', a rumor 'extremists' were trying to keep alive because they sought anarchy. Truth was, according to the upper castes who controlled government and commerce, Sikhs had always accepted the spiritual power structure that made gods of one caste and spiritual lepers of another.

With a sigh Banda recalled that after the upper castes had defeated the Sikhs, the Christians had become the new focus of assimilation. But total assimilation of the Christians didn't come as easy as the Sikhs and only came after the Collapse, in the newly formed Empire, Aryana, when the original Bible had been destroyed and a new Bible had taken its place, when a new Bible had been rewritten to incorporate caste as the divine spiritual glue of society, placing Athmans at the top and Brahmans at the bottom. The irony, Banda thought, was that the ruling castes who had stormed and shellacked the Golden Temple centuries ago had themselves been regulated to low castes by a small corporate elite using the same techniques of propaganda and assimilation that had been used on the original natives of the land. From his documents he understood that these corporate elite were themselves upper castes, but they simply did not wish to dilute or share their power with an entire caste that had grown too big for its own good. Banda could prove all this with his salvaged books. He could help free the Brahmans and the Shudra from physical and spiritual bondage. But he also knew that propaganda in the Empire was absolute. No matter what documents or books he possessed no one would ever believe that there was a time in history when the Brahmans were the living gods of society. Anyone who would say such a blasphemous thing would be made an example of. Thinking about what had happened to the Shudra and the Brahmans, Banda wondered if somehow the same thing would one day happen to the Athmans. He wondered if they too would be relegated to untouchability by an even smaller group of people who didn't want to share their power at the top of the caste hierarchy. He didn't want to think about the Athmans anymore, and he prayed that Caste Apartheid would be destroyed long before another caste would have the opportunity to emerge and usurp another.

Reaching the base of a small rocky mountain, Banda shook his head and felt a deep sadness for the Sikhs of the Empire who kept slaves and who denied the idea that Sikhs had ever banned Sati or Devadasi or fought against the upper castes or had ever forfeited their last names as one of the greatest acts of rebellion to Caste Apartheid. But they had, and the old librarian was collecting the history to prove it. If not for those in the Empire, for those outside in the Deadlands.

The upper castes hadn't destroyed all documents in the Sikh library when they had stormed the Golden Temple with their army. He had heard stories of a very courageous family that had escaped the temple just before the Sikh library was incinerated with all the irreplaceable artifacts and documents that proved Sikh rebellions to upper caste tyranny. He had heard that this family had kept these artifacts safe and intact for the last two hundred years but that now the Aryan-Athmans had found them and that they were transporting the artifacts back to Aryana to finish a job that had started centuries ago.

Banda could not allow it. He would not allow it. All those years protecting truth only to be destroyed now. He would risk it all to protect what these brave souls risked their lives to save.

But the outlaws Banda led didn't understand why they should risk their lives for mere books and artifacts that belonged to another time and place. They had been discussing the issue for the last few

17

hours while Banda silently listened. One outlaw said:
"We're on a fool's errand. We should turn back while we still have a chance. Risking our lives, for what? Old books. Books! Books that nobody cares about anymore…"

There was a collective sigh as they followed a serpentine trail up a mountain. Another outlaw added: "We could be doing so much more with our time. We could be helping slaves. We could be stealing provisions. We could be sabotaging their sonic trains. We could be destroying their K-Bongs and saving lives. But we're not doing any of that. Instead we're trying to rob a train with books and artifacts nobody really cares about anymore."

"I care," Banda said without looking back at his men. "Athmans care. Why else would they risk the operation if they did not care? Anyone who knows the value of history cares and--" Before he could finish the thought a sudden scream rent the silence. It came from afar and barely floated back to their ears; still everyone stopped in their tracks. A moment later it came again, and again, and then it stopped all at once. Everyone recognized the rhythm of the agony. Some poor man had been infected with rage beetles and the larvae were slowly digging their way out of his skull, popping out of his head one small scuttling beetle at a time. It was one of the most if not the most painful way to die in the Deadlands.

Utter silence reigned as Banda momentarily thought about all the genetically modified insects and monsters the Athmans had created with their science for their coliseums and entertainment. A lot of these chimeras roaming around the Deadlands reminded him of the creatures that had once existed before man, the creatures often referred to as 'dinosaurs' in the old books of his growing library.

18

For a moment Banda even wondered if the dinosaurs of long ago had themselves been remnants of a highly scientific society that had tampered with DNA, cloning, and ultimately destroyed itself with its cleverness. He even thought that perhaps these dinosaurs of long ago were products of the highly advanced Atlantis, and like the citizens of Atlantis the Aryans of Aryana were destined to destroy themselves.

"What value?" An outlaw blurted at last as they headed toward a small mountain village that had been looted and pillaged by Deadland scavengers; or worse, failed mutations and experiments of Aryana dumped outside the Great Wall with the rest of the trash. "The only thing worth fighting for is the future. What's done is done and cannot be changed. We are wasting our time with these artifacts."

Banda turned to him as he entered the village. "If it is true what you say…that there is no value in history," he answered meditatively, "then tyrants wouldn't spend all their time and resources trying to rewrite it." He went silent for a moment as he stepped over the skeletal remains of a chimera. "You want to change a people, change their history. Change a people's history and you change their future."

One outlaw repeated these words to himself. Change a people's history and you change their future.

After a few difficult steps over a mound of rotting flesh and corrupting skeletons, Banda covered his nose and added: "You are where you come from. If they manage to change where you come from, then they manage to change who you are and where you're going. The best way to fight for the future is to protect the past."

"The best way to fight for the future is to protect the past…" whispered a Brahman outlaw with the tattoos of an untouchable

19

and the brand of his former Athman master on his forehead. For a moment the outlaw remembered an untouchable friend he knew when he was a slave. She had maintained that Brahmans weren't always slaves and that there was a time when they could read and write, a time when they were even allowed to read and interpret the religious texts for themselves.

But not anymore.

The laws of Athman Society now maintained that because of some historical betrayal to an Athman ruler a thousand years ago the Brahmans were banned from reading and writing and were ordained slaves of the Athmans until they cleansed their souls and freed themselves from spiritual bondage through countless lives of dutiful service to the Athmans.

These laws of conduct for the Brahman slaves were even codified, and they were so severe that if any Brahman was caught walking on a path reserved for upper castes or if they were caught reading the religious texts of Athman Divine Society they would have boiling lead poured down their ears.

The Brahman outlaw had been forced to watch many of these public executions of poor Brahmans who had mistakenly used the wrong path, or made a wrong turn, or had mistakenly overheard the hymns of the sacred texts as they walked past an Athman Temple. He himself had been scheduled for execution for having worn sandals in front of an Athman 'god'. It was his luck that the Outlaws of the Dead had infiltrated the Empire and helped him and the other prisoners escape through one of the many secret 'trains'. Even the underground 'train movement' his friend had told him had been inspired by a historical event that had taken place centuries ago in a country that no longer existed. According to some slaves this historical betrayal of the Brahmans never really took place. It was a lie—a lie recently added to the religious texts and heavily propagated in the schools as if it had always been there. Some slaves claimed that not only had the Brahmans never betrayed the Athmans but the Athmans never even existed until the Empire was established.

Now the former slave thought about Banda's words and he was beginning to wonder if the past had been truly manipulated and rewritten to make gods of one people and slaves of another. There would be no real way of ever knowing. It just seemed like that's how it had always been and that Athmans ruling over everyone was as much cultural as it was religious. How could anyone really know? How could anyone determine what was true and what was not when the upper castes had total and complete control of history, education and the media, and, with these tools of manipulation and subjugation, control of thoughts, feelings and minds. The Athmans controlled, in the end, the future. A future dictated by the past, a past that may have very well been fabricated to keep a few in power. If this were true, if this were in fact the case, he would want to know. He would want to know if the Athmans had humiliated his people with their lies and history.
"So what are we trying to remember?" said another slave of the Empire who also owed his freedom to Sundri and her outlaws. "That it all went to shit!"

"Not that it went to shit but 'how' it went to shit," Banda answered, staring down at the skeletal remains of a humanoid with fangs and claws—a creation of the Empire no doubt for their coliseum. "The 'how' is what we are concerned with. Not the result, the causes. For if we know the 'how' we can prevent it from repeating in the future, and maybe one day we can finally put an end to Caste Apartheid."

21

"So how? I mean you're sitting on a library of salvaged books, aren't you? You must have some idea." He was referring to Banda's home, where he was slowly restoring the ruins of Nalanda, an ancient university that had been restored before the Collapse and decimated during the Great War.

Banda answered without looking back. "I do," he said. "I have an idea." He thought about his words, then continued with slight pauses to concentrate on the craggy terrain beneath his feet. "These ruling caste tyrants have been gods for centuries, and they have been so because they are very clever at their oppression; they share it and hide it and that is why their tyranny is so difficult to overthrow. The real question is: how are the upper castes able to assimilate so cleverly and for so long and to do so despite the most blatant rebellions to their hierarchy? How is it that every time there is a rebellion against caste no one remembers? Not now, not ever. It's erased from history or recorded as though it never happened, or as though the rebellion was about something else. You're made to believe that the rebellion was about everything else but caste. Everyone thinks it was about this or that but never about what it really was—ending caste oppression." He laughed to himself. "Today there is barely a trace of the memory that Buddhism and Sikhism were direct reactions and rebellions to caste oppression. Barely a trace. Not a single memory. How is it that Judaism and Christianity now embrace caste as if caste society had always been part of their religious thinking? It wasn't always the case, and yet citizens of the Empire believe it was, believe it always was. Citizens believe caste is history and the great tradition of the land when it is nothing of the kind. It is propagated as such to make citizens believe it cannot be changed—to foster a kind of indifference and complacency."

Banda went silent for a moment, then he continued: "Caste Apartheid is the foulest form of physical and spiritual oppression ever known to man and yet it has survived even when so many other forms of tyranny were killed. What's the difference between other apartheids and this one? Others are perceived as manmade. Caste apartheid is taught and perceived as spiritual, religious, and belonging to all religions. What's the difference between Hitler's Aryan and the ruling caste Aryan? Same idea, except one was put down, and the other thrived. Why? Why would the world fight against one oppression while ignore the other?"

No one answered and it could have been because many of the outlaws didn't know who Hitler was. Sometimes Banda took for granted the history he knew, especially history from the old world. After a moment Banda supplied an answer:

"One tyrant changed history and religion and made it seem like culture and unchangeable spiritual doctrine at the same time. The other didn't, or was stopped before they could, as they surely would have as Hitler had openly emulated the upper castes in the creation of his Aryan ideal. How is the Nazi Aryan different from the Athman Aryan? There is no real difference. Down the line they are the same. One believes in a noble and pure race that makes them Supermen, the other believes in a noble and pure caste that makes them living gods. Same idea. Same arrogance. Same oppression. Only the Athmans made us all believe it has always been this way in the land and that it is divine law found in every religion…making us believe that karma and reincarnation are cultural and belong to all religions, confusing citizens by using the words 'caste' and 'varma' interchangeably when they are not at all the same. They made us believe that it was always accepted and never questioned or rebelled against; and yet, the truth is caste tyranny has been the greatest source of rebellion for the last thousands of years in this very area and there is absolutely no record of it. Caste oppression has been greatest source of rebellion in the land! And yet you would never believe it by reading their history. By reading their history you would think the greatest source of tyranny was Islamic crusades of conversion. But they are nothing, really, in comparison to the oppression and tyranny of the upper castes."

Banda laughed at the absurdity of how propaganda could distort so much and create within citizens a whole new sensibility not to mention a feeling of complacency and helplessness. If no one has rebelled against caste, if not one has ever died for spiritual freedom, and if caste has always been an accepted part of the land why should I try to change anything.

"Athmans didn't even exist before the Collapse! They didn't! Yet everyone believes they have existed since the dawn of time. This is incredible to me. Caste itself is not very old. Varma yes, but not caste as we know it. Yet everyone believes caste as it is now has been there since the beginning of time. It hasn't. Varma, yes. But not caste, not Caste Apartheid. And there is a difference. Caste Apartheid is varma rewritten by the upper castes to place them in power, to make them gods, and to make living slaves of every other caste. It was never like this before. By god, I swear it." There was a short silence. No one said anything, but they didn't have to. Banda knew these outlaws didn't really know the difference between varma and caste and that he was getting ahead of himself. The words were constantly mixed up by the upper caste scholars to mix up the people and create a sense that they were the same thing. But they weren't the same thing. Not remotely, and yet so-called intellectuals of the Empire used the words interchangeably. After a moment Banda explained:

"A long time ago there was a social system called varma. There was nothing religious or binding about varma. Varma was simply a way to categorize jobs in society. Tradesman. Priest. Warrior. There were three varmas and no hierarchy, and there was a lot of free movement and inter-marrying between the varmas. A warrior could marry a tradesman, a priest could marry a warrior. A tradesman could become a priest and a priest could become a tradesman. Then comes a group that wants to take control of society through religion; so they change the word varma to make it religious. They adopt another name to slowly change the definition to support their rule. They adopt the Portuguese word 'caste' and decide 'caste' replaces varma. They also decide that caste is hierarchal supported by two religious doctrines of karma and reincarnation as interpreted and defined by the priests."

Banda stopped, realizing the outlaws probably didn't know what he meant by Portuguese. When no one asked, he continued: "The upper castes support and justify this idea of caste hierarchy through religious doctrines of reincarnation and karma that was never a part of varma, and they put the fear of offending or going against the upper castes in all the texts and stories of the land. Then they do another thing. Then they create a new caste for the dark skinned natives of the land. From three free and interdependent varmas based on occupation to four rigid and religious castes based on karma and reincarnation that has everyone serving the upper castes for a better birth in the next life. The first three castes they call the Aryan castes, the slave caste they call the Shudra untouchables, and they exist to serve the three noble castes hand and foot."

Banda paused to collect his thoughts. Not many outlaws

knew that the addition of hierarchy and the untouchable caste was
a relatively new addition to the ancient varma system that never
oppressed or put one trade over another. He also realized that
the upper castes had not only redefined varma but karma as well.
At one time karma meant the good and bad deeds one did in the
course of one life. Once the upper castes had appropriated the
word, karma came to mean all the good and bad deeds one did for
the Aryans and their system of control. Anyone who went against
caste or the ruling castes were promised a lower birth in the next
life while those who blindly protected and served the ruling castes
and their apartheid were promised spiritual evolution.

It was spiritual tyranny at its best. Creating new definitions for old words that were considered part of the land was their
strength as tyrants. Lesser tyrants would have tried to create new
words along with new definitions. New words could easily be
overthrown and forgotten. But not words that were already part of
the very fabric of society. Not words that were crushed and assimilated like the religions of the land by the great Aryan boa constrictor. Assimilated words with slightly different yet similar definitions
were harder to reject or rebel against. There was no greater tyrant
in the history of the world than the Aryan tyrant and there was
no older system of spiritual slavery and oppression than Caste
Apartheid. With a struggle Banda climbed over a rocky incline and
continued:

"The Aryans create a new caste for the dark skinned natives of the land in order to create slaves. And these slaves, these
untouchables are treated worse than animals but not worse than
foreigners who might observe their system of tyranny and try
to destroy it from the outside. In their hierarchy foreigners are
dismissed as lower than the low castes, lower even than animals

born in the Empire, and they are called lechers, and if untouchables don't serve the Aryans properly in this life they risk being reborn a foreign lecher in the next life. The whole system thrives on promises for the afterlife. Heaven is rising up the ladder. Hell is descending. It's not doing good or bad deeds. It's doing good or bad deeds in in accordance to what the Aryan masters say is good or bad."

Banda shook his head at the system the upper castes had crafted and evolved over the centuries. They had given everyone something to lose should their system be destroyed. Every caste below served the one above in some way, shape or form; and every Aryan could make a slave out of an untouchable. They were the universal slaves to the Aryans. Thinking about this clever system crafted so almost anyone with power or influence had something to lose should caste be destroyed, Banda continued:

"Since no one else but the upper castes can read the texts, the texts begin to change over the centuries to support and justify their hierarchy. Anyone that contradicts caste is savagely put down and their rebellion recorded in history as a rebellion to anything else but caste and this changing of facts and history is done to hide their oppression and avoid drawing unnecessary attention to their apartheid. This goes on until the Collapse. At this time caste changes again and the corporate elite create a new caste, a new god, and they usurp the old gods, doing to them what they had done to the original dark skinned natives of the land. They change all texts to reflect this new caste and then they incite the Aryan Reclamation to assimilate the last of the old Christians and Jews as they had done with the Sikhs and the Buddhists long ago."

He sighed at what had happened during the Aryan Reclamation. Thousands of Christians and Jews exterminated and the young assimilated so that they could add caste, karma, and jati to their religious doctrines without much if any protest. Anyone who knew any better had disappeared. Those who were left were young and could be molded to believe something slightly different. Now the only Christians and Jews who still believed in the old versions of their respective religions were persecuted outlaws living in the Deadlands. After a silence, Banda added:

"Now more than a third of society is in a state of slavery because of this rewriting of history that begins when social varma was transformed to religious caste by the upper castes...when the original dark-skin natives of the land were deemed untouchable and made slaves in their own homes. That's why we're on this mission. Our 'how' is: how do we reverse centuries of lies and half-truths and return dignity to the original dark-skinned natives of the land? To the Christians? Muslims? Jews? Buddhists? Brahmans? Sikhs? How do we turn Cast Apartheid back to the original varma system? That's our 'how'? And that will be our victory. The utter destruction of slavery and Caste Apartheid once and for all."

The outlaws were silent and thoughtful as they followed the old librarian through the ruins. The old librarian of Nalanda knew so much about upper caste tyranny and history that they had nothing to say or add. If even half of what of what he had just told them was true, rescuing any document to bring them closer to the truth was worth the risk.

Just as the outlaws approached the side of the mountain one outlaw began to cough violently and had to stop for medicine. Everyone stopped and waited for him as he reached into his pocket and pulled out a jug. The outlaw had a growth in his left lung that would easily be cured with a little AX. Banda watched the outlaw, nodded knowingly, and said:

"Do you know that just a century ago your cough would have been a death sentence? They didn't call it a plague at the time, but it was a plague, and no one should ever forget the sacrifice Seva made for us."

The outlaw took his medicine. His coughing stopped almost instantly, and they all continued up a narrow trail in the growing heat of day. After a short silence the old librarian told them the story of how Seva dared to challenge and undermine the corporate gods to save the world from the unofficial plague.

*

In the old times before the Reclamation, when the world still hadn't been divided into republic and empire, and the mighty corporations ruled over governments like mighty gods, there was a man who lived in the surrounding slums of the city with his son. The man's name was Udam Singh, but his nickname was Seva; for Seva meant charity in his language and he had been called Seva by his friends because he was always looking out for the welfare of others; always doing what he could to help those in need even though he himself lived in impoverished circumstances. Seva hadn't always been poor, or living in the slums, but when his wife incurred the plague everything changed. The doctors, or rather the medical merchants as he liked to call them, relieved him of his wealth in exchange for a treatment they claimed might save her from a painful and humiliating sickness that was killing one-in-three citizens.

But the expensive treatments did nothing for Seva's wife; if anything they made her condition worse, destroying her from the inside out, prolonging her suffering along with the profit her

pain afforded the medical merchants who had prolonged her in-
evitable death until they had taken Seva for everything. When after
months of indescribable suffering his wife died, Seva had no choice
but to move out of the walled cities of the corporate gods and into
the slums of man that would eventually come to be known as the
Deadlands. There in the place that would come to be known as the
Deadlands he met so many ill-fated souls with similar situations
and stories; and there in the Deadlands he had heard a strange and
terrible rumor that the 'medicine' the medical merchants were
selling was not a cure or treatment but a terrible poison that destroyed every last natural defense the body had. He had heard that
before the highly corrosive 'medicine' had ever been pushed like
heroine by the medical merchants the plague was not a plague at
all but a rare occurrence that more often than not went away on its
own. The 'treatment' or the 'medicine' decimated the immunity so
that the only hope and chance to kill the plague was the unafford-
able 'medicine' the government had been subsidizing it couldn't
anymore. More often than not the plague would disappear and
patients would wither away and die as a result of all the damage
inflicted by the treatments the medical merchants were claiming
was the only hope to fight the plague.

A decade prior to his wife's slow and painful death the
plague was hardly a plague and killed maybe one-in-twenty citizens. A decade later, one-in-three, and Seva could see two major
things had changed. First, medicine that could save lives could
be patented for profit by the corporate gods. Second, health and
safety measures imposed by governments on all products had
relaxed to the point of nonexistence as the corporate gods silently
took over government and began to change policy that protected
the public and undermined their profit. With the loss of safety

measures and regulatory boards, cities soon became contaminated with radioactive products that mutated cells over prolonged periods of use while the food supply suffered from the same contamination with processed commodity crops that were cheap and fast to grow but that without genetic modifications were poisonous to the public. To sell more processed corn and crop, the same diet to fatten pigs was pushed by the government as safe and healthful to the public.

Everything was done for the corporate gods and their power which they measured in profit.

Within ten or so years, everything sold was about fifty percent processed poison and all electronics had enough lithium to blow up a vault. Within ten or so years, one-in-twenty became one-in-three and some corporate gods suddenly realized they could profit from the disease with ineffective treatments they had patented and that and been designed to create a dependency and prolong life for profit. And some people even believed that the contamination of the food supply with genetically modified cash crops or the lithium floating around in everyone's pocket was not the culprit. Some actually believed it was the toxic treatments themselves. Medical merchants were quick at the draw, quick to diagnose, quick to incite fear, quick to sell more treatments that would further reduce a person's health and immunity. Before the toxic treatments had been pushed by the medical merchants only one-in-twenty died of plague, and the plague was nothing more than a simple abnormality the body could—given the chance— heal on its own. The treatment robbed the body of that chance. So one-in-twenty become one-in-three and the medical merchants and the corporate gods were all the richer for it.

That was not all Seva discovered.

Seva also met many shunned and exiled doctors who had told him the medicine the infected were being given by the medical merchants had never once been proven effective in any kind of clinical test and that on the contrary had almost certainly been proven to be disastrous to the body. They told him those that it supposedly 'cured' would have been 'cured' anyway. They even told him that more often than not the medicine was the cause of death and not the plague, and the more treatments they gave the patient the weaker and weaker the patient got until the body could do little more than shrivel up and wither away.

But this medicine made profit unimaginable for the mighty corporate gods, especially the pharmaceutical god Thaiyser. Thaiyser took good care of his minions, and the medical merchants who pushed the radioactive poison to the sick and all those who worked for Thaiyser got to live fat, comfortable lives behind the walls of Thaiyser City. Any doctor who went against Thaiyser disappeared; or was imprisoned; or worse yet, was ridiculed by the god Medea who controlled all the tastes, thoughts and opinions of citizens with her opinion making machinations. If there was one thing that could be admired about the gods, it was that they stood strong and together against their subjects.

All these rumors and conspiracies shattered Seva's sensibilities so that when his son fell sick and died because he had been exposed to the radioactive 'treatments' his mother had been receiving, Seva vowed an oath to prevent such things from happening to any other family.

Lost and alone, searching for answers, Seva set out on a long journey through the dying lands and slums of the world to find truth. And every year his heart grew heavier and heavier with immeasurable sadness as he met hundreds of unfortunate souls who had suffered dearly at the hands of the merchants and gods. And every year on the anniversary of his son's death he swore an oath that he would stop this madness and that he would make the world a better place not just for a few, but for all—

For all and not just those who had sold their souls to the new gods.

And so after ten years of endless searching, the truth finally found him. It was while he was trekking through the Deadlands that he came upon an old man lying unconscious in the dirt road. The man had long white hair; his face was scarred and burnt by the unforgiving sun and relentless wind. His eyes were dark and alert, and he wore the rags of a scavenger which were soaked in his blood. He had been stabbed, robbed, and left on the road to be crushed by a transport truck. When Seva pulled him out of the road to safety, he told the old man his story as he dressed his stomach wounds. He told the scavenger how his wife had died of plague; how he had sold everything he had to help her with a treatment that not only killed her but his son as well; and he told him how he had vowed to make sure no family would ever have to experience what he had experienced.

When Seva finally finished his story the old man gazed at him in amazement and disbelief, forgetting the sharp pains in his stomach. It was as though he were staring at a living miracle.

At last the old scavenger spoke, telling Seva that he was convinced fate had somehow brought them together, telling him that he was a doctor, a real doctor and that he had once possessed the cure for the plague and that he had possessed it decades before there had ever been such a thing as a plague that mutated cells in the body. The keen doctor then told Seva how the cure he had possessed was commonly used for other problems and how it got rid of the plague without inflicting any damage to the health or immune system of the infected. Then he sighed and told Seva that the only problem with the cure was a financial one. The new gods could not patent the formula as it had been around for many years before treatments and cures for deadly diseases could be patented and exploited for profit. It had in essence been around since Louis Pasteur had discovered penicillin and had gifted it to humanity. He then continued his story and told Seva how he had been ridiculed and exiled by the medical merchants and how the cure was subsequently wiped from shelves until the gods could figure out a way to own it. But the cure was so common no one could patent the formula that was commonly known as Ambrosia X. So the great god Thaiyser did the only thing he could do. With the help of his demi-gods and minions, he did all he could to erase the very memory of this cheap and accessible cure that would undermine his power. The doctor then added that he was the last living memory of AX and that he was hiding from Thaiyser's minions who sought to eliminate him as the last living threat to their beloved god. This, of course, infuriated Seva, and, the rage blood pounding in his head, he could hardly pay attention to the old doctor as he explained how Thaiyser had destroyed every last trace of AX and had kept the formula protected in a fortified tower waiting for the day they could reintroduce the cure as their own.

When the doctor was finished his story, Seva thanked him and told him he would do all he could to make things right again. So saying, he journeyed to Thaiyser City and bravely marched up to Thaiyser's minions. Without fear or hesitation he demanded the public be made aware of the existence of the real cure and savagely accused them of mass murder. But the god's minions laughed at him, dismissed him as mad, and then secretly tried to silence him with many bribes, offering him riches untold if he would lead them to the last real doctor who had 'lied' to him about AX. But when Seva wouldn't be silenced, when he wouldn't be bribed, they did to him as they had done with the doctor. They sent their very assassins after him. But Seva hiding in the sewers and alleys of the opulent city escaped every assassination attempt. Just as he was about to escape the city, a strange thing happened. A Thaisyer minion, a medicinal merchant who had once been a real doctor found him, rushed up to him and whispered in his ear the secret location of the hidden formula, adding that he was sorry for all he had done and that there were many repentant medical merchants just like him who dreamed of one day being real doctors again. Then, as he told Seva where he could find these rebel merchants, an assassin's bullet shook the night and within seconds the redeemed merchant collapsed to the ground dead.

With this new information, Seva found the other rebels and they agreed to help him steal the cure from the gods for the people. And so, Seva, with the help of the rebels, made his way up the mountain of Thaiyser where he fought and defeated Thaiyser security forces. Fighting his way to the top, he finally reached the tower where they kept the cure. With a phone he had turned into a bomb, he blasted the vault that held the cure, and, taking the secret formula, he dashed out of the tower, rushed down the mountain, and escaped the city with hundreds of Thaiyser minions in pursuit.

Once out of harm's way, Seva quickly took the formula to the doctor and together they posted the formula on rebel-net, the underground internet the gods could not control or shut down. Within moments it was in the hands of thousands; within hours the formula was viral; and within months the plague had been reduced to nothing more than a common cold. Once the plague was no more, citizens and non-citizens alike turned their anger and hate toward Thaisyer, and they did what no one ever thought possible—

They killed a god.

When the other gods had discovered what had happened to their fellow god, they panicked, and in bitter retaliation, sent out all their forces against Seva.

For the longest time they couldn't find him. The non-citizens of the slums stuck together and were able to keep Seva safe from their wrath. But one day, as was to be expected, Seva was betrayed by a close friend for a better life and opportunity as a corporate citizen in a corporate city of his choosing.

With Seva captured, the gods brought him before their court where they agreed a televised execution would be insufficient. Seva had stolen from them, he had stolen from the gods and he would not only have to pay, he would have to be made an example of. No one would ever dare to steal from a god after they were through with him.

And so they submitted him to the 'Akali Project' to show the world what they could do with their power and knowledge. With their science and technology they altered Seva's genetic code so that he could heal and regenerate as quickly and easily as taking a breath. Then they operated on his brain and slowed down his internal clock so that he would only age one minute every century. When Seva had been augmented to practical immortality, they carried his beaten and tortured body up to the highest skyscraper in the city. There, for all to see, they chained him to the shiny metal roof to be cooked by sun and picked at by the crows and vultures until the end of time. And to this very day Seva remains

there, chained to the highest skyscraper in Aryana suffering countless agonies so that no other husband or father would have to.

*

The outlaws were silent as they pushed up the trail through the
hills. Each one thought of the story the old librarian had just
related to them. Some thought about the medical merchants and
how they had betrayed their life's purpose by putting profit before
the people they swore to protect. Some thought about Seva and
his sacrifice and wondered if they could ever make such a sacrifice.
Some had never seen the corporate elite as gods, and saw how, yes,
they could be viewed as the new gods of society, or, in the very
least, the new kings. Others wondered what they would do if they
had lost their families to a plague that could have been treated as
nothing more than a common cold. Another thought about Aryan
bio-technology and how the Athmans had discovered a way to
slow down the biological clock while at the same time accelerating
healing and tissue regeneration. Only the Athmans were allowed
to undergo the process of the immortal; the social ramifications
of citizens living thousands of years--even if they belonged to
an Aryan caste--was hard if not impossible to manage. It would
become a logistic nightmare for the few Athmans who controlled
society. It was rumored that this science was not new science and
that the corporate elite had already been alive for thousands of
years so that those who turned the original dark skinned natives of
the land into slaves and those who recently turned Brahmans into
slaves were one and the same. Athman immortality was why they
were able to adapt and evolve their tyranny to the changing times.
It was why Caste Apartheid was so well protected and established.

The Athmans had thousands of years of experience protecting and maintaining their power structure which they changed and patched and weaved into culture and religion as culture and religion demanded. Nothing that challenged the living gods would be allowed to exist or to be remembered. That was the rule, the only rule, the rule that allowed them to maintain their apartheid for as long as they had, and they made sure it was enforced by sword and by pen.

When Varma needed to be religious it was renamed Caste and supported by spiritual laws of karma and reincarnation that empowered the self-proclaimed living gods of society. When it needed to be cultural to survive it was referred to as Varma and soon the Aryan intellectuals were merging the two words into one, mixing the whole thing up, claiming that Varma-Caste had always been a part of the land without drawing attention to the fact that Varma and Caste were like apples and oranges. They were not the same thing, yet they were treated as the same thing, treated by the ruling caste intellectuals, the only ones allowed to write for hundreds of years, as the same thing. Varma permitted freedom of movement and marriage among three equal varmas. Caste banned this. Caste was another animal altogether. Caste added a category to enslave natives in a hierarchy based on karma points that could be earned by these 'spiritual lepers' so that they too could rise up the caste ladder in the next life if they simply respected and treated the ruling castes as living gods in the current life. In future lives they would get to reincarnate up the caste ladder. That was the 'divine' promise. But for the current life they should be content with abject slavery and not try to change or challenge ruling caste society otherwise they would lose karma points and reincarnate down the caste ladder. There was nothing cultural about caste.

Caste was 'religion' as penned and interpreted by the ruling castes for their society.

When the Buddhists and Sikhs and Christians maintained they had never subscribed to such 'spiritual' laws that made slaves or gods of citizens, that to was changed and with the exact same formula: the ruling castes exterminated the older generation that remembered truth; incinerated any and all facts that ever mentioned rebellion to caste; then they assimilated a lost, confused and shattered younger generation by making them absolute experts in a slightly altered version of the old religion; and forever they would be too busy fighting with themselves to focus their attention on real tyranny and oppression; and forever they would embrace caste as varma and say caste had always been a part of the land. When the truth was the greatest lie and evil ever presented as religion was caste. Caste, not varma. And there was a difference, a big difference, and one day everyone in the Empire would know the evil of Caste Apartheid.

Banda turned to regard the outlaws. Their eyes shone with history and appreciation for Seva's sacrifice and he could see they were muttering inward prayers for Seva who was still chained high up on the highest skyscraper in Aryana. He was just about to relate another story about a forgotten hero who dared to go up against the corporate gods when a shriek followed by a series of screams rent the night and sent a shiver through his bones. Banda stopped suddenly, and raised his hand to warn the outlaws. Instantly, the outlaws withdrew their weapons and halted as Banda eased toward the ridge. He stopped when he reached the edge. Down in the valley he watched in horror as a group of thugees plundered a small settlement of free slaves. Thugees rushed in and out of canvas tents and caravans pulling out clothes, tools, and food while the free slaves ran, crawled, begged and screamed in frantic flight.

The thugees were menacing figures. Clad in black human hide, and brandishing dull iron tridents they butchered all without mercy. Banda knew these poor men and women didn't have a chance and that, sadly, their initial mistake had likely been compassion. Thugees played on compassion and trust to facilitate reconnaissance. One of their members, usually a child, had infiltrated the settlement, pretending to have been the sole survivor of some made-up attack; when the young mole had learned everything about the settlement, the toughest and bravest of the settlement were either poisoned or executed in their sleep so that the band of thugs could raid the settlement without much resistance. In the old world the British had tried to exterminate the thugees but somehow they managed to survive and now in the Deadlands they thrived.

Banda sighed and watched the thugees as they rounded up the youngest of the children which they would assimilate into their band, lying to them about how they were found, creating a history for them that would afford their band the greatest loyalty. The poor children who were old enough to remember the raid were exterminated with the rest.

Banda closed his eyes and muttered a silent prayer. A moment later he opened eyes dark eyes, transformed into a deadly and silent lion, poised to attack these butchers. He withdrew his bow and nocked a gold-tipped arrow as the outlaws held their swords at the ready. Just when he was about to down a thug with an arrow to signal the attack, he was startled by a clicking sound and the tumbling of collapsing rocks and pebbles. From above a young girl threatened:

"One move and I shoot, old man!"

For a moment Banda could scarcely believe he had been called an old man, then he turned and looked up at a young girl aiming some sort of assault rifle at him. She was barely twelve with the brand of a slave tattooed across her face. The rifle in her hands was a makeshift combination of salvaged rifles from the old world. He wondered if the rifle worked; or if it would possibly jam and explode in her hands like a ross rifle. He looked around the sun-lit mountain to see if she was alone and quickly observed another shadow moving about the rocks.

A smaller shadow.

Another child, perhaps.

Banda guessed they were waiting for the thugs to finish their dark work and leave so they could salvage whatever had been left behind.

Banda didn't want to hurt this child, but he needed to get to the settlement below before the thugs finished their dark work. As a Sikh of Old he just could not turn his back on these poor people, even if it meant his own life. Without fear or hesitation, he turned to face the girl, aiming his arrow at her hand. He warned: "Your gun might jam. My arrow won't. Drop your weapon, child, and walk away!"

She answered his threat with a smile; then she whistled loud. Within seconds a dozen or so children emerged from hiding, pointing rifles at him.

"One move and they shoot, old man!"